THE CASE OF THE DISAPPEARING FIANCÉ

SURPRISING SHORELINE SECRETS SURFACE IN BURLYBOTTOM

PIPPA FINN MYSTERIES
BOOK NINE

POPPY BLYTHE

PUREREAD.COM

CONTENTS

DEAR READER, GET READY FOR ANOTHER GREAT COZY...

READY TO SOLVE THE MYSTERY?

Turn the page and let's begin

❦

1

Pippa awoke with a heavy heart, as she had done every day since the incident. The image of Clive falling from the top of St. Paul's Cathedral was burned into her mind. He was there, falling and she tried to save him, but she was out of reach. He had died protecting her, his last act, one of bravery, and she wondered if this was enough to erase all of the other moments of cowardice in his life. She had stood there at the barrier, looking down as the cluster of people rushed around the broken, fallen bodies, trying to avoid the scarlet pool that trickled out. Jack had held her, pulling her close into him and twisting her head so that it was buried in his chest and she didn't have to look at the grisly sight any longer, but it was already too late.

After that there was the funeral, a service where a lot of people attended, but most of them didn't stay for long.

They were there because they thought they ought to be there, not because they really wanted to. Pippa had wept for a man whose heart she had broken, a man who she had left because their lives did not match up any longer. She cursed him for being so bitter that he fell in with a villain, and stood there as an innocent woman was murdered. She mourned him when she thought about the way he used to make her laugh, or how she used to picture their lives together.

Months had passed since then. Pippa was mostly able to put on a brave face and cope with the rigors of the world. Because of the new will that had been uncovered, and Pippa's decision to not contest it, the cottage had been sold and the contents went to an auction house, with the proceeds going to the children's hospital in Poland. Pippa knew that they were more deserving of the money than she was. She still had plenty left in the bank thanks to her financial endeavours with Clive. But it did leave her homeless. Jack had stepped in and told her that she could stay on the farm with him. There was an extension to the house that had once been a barn, but was converted into living quarters. It was separated from the main farm house by its own door, so it was almost like a semi-detached house. She could still have her independence, but it also meant that Jack was not far away. Pippa had welcomed this show of support and compassion, and had not hesitated in taking him up on his offer. In the months that had passed since, she had not tried to find another place to live as she did not wish to be alone again, at least not yet.

But something had changed within her as well. Clive's death had affected her deeply, and although she wanted to make her relationship with Jack evolve, it had not happened yet. It felt as though there was a stain on her soul and she was not quite sure how to cleanse it. It wasn't as though there wasn't anything to look forward to; after all, she was still Callie's maid of honor and the preparations for the wedding were going well, but there was a sense of disquiet in Pippa's life, and she was simply waiting for it to end.

She left her room and went into the farm house for dinner. She and Jack had a routine of cooking for each other, and often spent the evenings eating together. Jasper already had a bowl of food prepared as Jack never forgot him. Pippa breathed in the smell of roasted meat and vegetables, and picked up her cutlery to begin eating.

"How are you today?" Jack asked. Pippa usually brushed off the question, but today she felt like being more honest.

"It's been six months since it happened. I feel like I should be over it by now. I feel like it shouldn't matter this much, but I still wake up thinking about him."

"You cared for him at one point. It's only natural to mourn."

"I keep telling myself that he was a bad person and I shouldn't let myself get so upset over it."

Jack looked at her plainly. "He wasn't a bad person Pippa, he just made some mistakes. It can happen to the best of us. If he was truly a bad person then he wouldn't have done what he did at the end. He protected you. I'll always be thankful to him for that."

"Maybe that's why it's so hard," Pippa said after thinking for a moment. "If he had been evil then it might make it easier to let him go. I just can't help thinking that some of this was my fault. If I hadn't left him so suddenly... if I had tried to make the break up go more smoothly then he might not have been so bitter toward me."

"The worst thing you can do is try and blame yourself for what happened. As much as I wish it could be so, you're never going to be able to go back and change the past. There was a time when I lost myself in those kinds of thoughts. After Emily died I kept thinking if there was something else I could have done or said, something to make things different. The truth is that there's nothing. All we can do is accept that sometimes things are out of our control," he said this with a shrug. It was rare that Jack would talk about his experiences with Emily, but Pippa had noticed he was becoming more forthcoming with sharing his feelings. She enjoyed seeing this sensitive, vulnerable side to him, even though it was difficult to talk about the people they had lost.

"How did you manage to escape the trap?"

Jack grinned. "It had a lot to do with your grandfather. A lot of people shared their condolences with me, but most people were content to let me mourn in peace. Gordon wasn't. He used to bring Jasper by here for a walk, and he would always say that Jasper liked this farm more than anywhere else in the town so he hoped that I didn't mind him bothering him. At first I just grunted and waited until he left, but that man was nothing if not persistent. Eventually he sat me down and he told me that it was going to hurt for a long time, but I couldn't keep thinking about what happened because I would never be able to change it. He said that in life we have to move on, even from the bad things, because otherwise we're never going to meet what's waiting around the corner for us. It was hard to hear, and it still took me a long time to listen to those words properly, but they made sense to me. He also told me that I shouldn't be too sad that she was gone because she wasn't the one who was in pain; I was. I was the one who suffered on her behalf, and that helped a lot as well. Emily made the most out of life, and that was the example I had to follow. I can't always say that I do live up to that example, but it's certainly something that I try to do. You'll get there as well. There's no timeline on grief. There's no way it should work. Everyone reacts differently, and it's always going to hit harder when you've been through something like what you went through. Seeing them fall like that... I'm not sure it's anything I'm going to forget."

"I keep thinking back to that moment and wondering if I could have moved more quickly, or reached out a little farther."

Jack shook his head. "Neither of us could have done anything Pippa. That's life. Sometimes there are things that you just can't help no matter how much you want to. In the end we are the powerless ones, and there are so many things out of our control."

"Doesn't that scare you though?"

He looked into her eyes and breath caught in her throat as she lost herself in his ice blue gaze. "It's all in the Lord's hands, and He'll take care of us, even when life is difficult." Jack spoke earnestly, and Pippa believed him with all her heart.

The situation was a little different for her, of course. When Jack had lost Emily they had been engaged to be married and Jack loved that woman with all his heart. The same couldn't be said for Pippa and Clive. Their relationship had long been on the rocks, but despite this Pippa still felt a sense of responsibility for it all, and she felt that since nobody else was going to mourn Clive then the onus was on her to try and remember him. Despite his faults she tried to picture him as the man he would have liked to be, rather than the one who made all those mistakes that ultimately led to his death.

The evening was still light and so after Pippa had finished with dinner she decided to go for a walk to clear her head.

Jasper certainly wasn't going to turn down the opportunity either. She fetched his leash and he bounded out of the door, tongue lolling out happily, his eyes gleaming with bright excitement.

Pippa's path took her along the seafront back toward the cottage. It was an aimless walk, and by the time she reached the cottage her thoughts had wandered so much that she was surprised she had arrived there. Outside the cottage was an unmarked white van, while loud noises emerged from inside the building. But Pippa was stopped as Mindy and Martha poked their heads out of their door and beckoned Pippa to come toward them. The two sisters cast wary glances at the cottage and they wore waspish looks on their faces as Pippa strolled down the garden path toward them.

"Evening Mindy, Martha," Pippa said politely. She had found that the two women were far more pleasant to talk with now that they were not living next door to her. Pippa didn't have to worry about them prying into her every movement.

"Do you know anything about the person who bought the cottage?" Mindy asked.

Pippa shrugged and put her hands on her hips, while Jasper investigated a nearby flowerbed. "Can't say that I do. Once I realized I couldn't afford to buy it, I stopped paying attention to it. It was completely out of my hands. I'm surprised that you don't know more about them."

"He seems to be a man of mystery. He's barely been here, and when he has he comes at all hours of the night and he hasn't made himself known. I mean, really, where are the manners? You would think he would know it's common courtesy to introduce himself to us," Mindy said. Pippa wondered if they were more aggrieved that they hadn't been able to glean any information about him rather than being insulted by the lack of courtesy.

"I'm sure he's just been busy. Moving is a very stressful thing," Pippa didn't think that Mindy and Martha would be aware of this. As far as she knew they had lived in the same cottage all their lives. They did not seem convinced of Pippa's reasoning either.

"Well, it's just not right. And all this building work he's got going on... I think he's changing the entire house. He shouldn't be allowed to do that. There's a reason why things in Burlybottom have not changed," Martha said.

"Well I'm sure if you have any concerns he'd be happy to listen to them, but as I said I really have no knowledge of him. It's not my cottage any longer," the words stuck in Pippa's throat. She had worked so diligently to protect her grandfather's legacy and get to the bottom of this treasure that he had left her. The search had been a long and arduous one, but eventually she had gotten to the root of it, only to find that the treasure hadn't been meant for her at all. She could have contested the old will, but she was sure that Granddad wouldn't have wanted this. Besides, the funds from the sale of the cottage would go a long way to helping the sick children in the hospital. However, it was difficult to look at the cottage and not see it as home. It was strange really, because when she had arrived in Burlybottom on Sea she had been disgusted by the state of the cottage as it was far from the luxury apartment she had lived in, in London.

"Well, I hope that things settle down soon enough. I don't like not knowing who our neighbor is," Mindy said.

"It's not right. We're a community here and people should understand that, before they move in. It's such a shame that you couldn't have stayed Pippa," Martha added. Pippa nodded, although she suppressed a smile. She distinctly remembered the sisters taking umbrage with her when she arrived because they were wary of her. They simply did not like change, but Pippa was sure that whoever this man was he would have his hands full with them trying to figure out who he was.

"I'm sure the building work will be finished sooner rather than later, and next time you see your neighbor you should invite him in for a cup of tea and show him the Burlybottom way." Pippa left them with a wide smile, although Martha and Mindy did not seem convinced with her advice.

Pippa walked back up the path and walked the short distance to stand outside the cottage. Scaffolding had been erected outside the cottage and the place had literally been turned into a building site. It was almost unrecognizable, and she thought it a shame that as soon as it had been sold someone had come along and thought they could improve the building. Yes it was old, and the inside had been covered with creaking floorboards, but it had a certain charm about it that was undeniable, at least to Pippa. Perhaps that was where the weakness of sentimentality came into things, though. Whoever had bought the cottage did not have the years of visits that Pippa had, and did not have any emotions tied to this place.

It might have been for the best, she realized, to allow this place to have a new lease on life. Still, it was a reminder of how things could drastically change and that all the years Gordon had spent in this place were no more.

Husky voices drifted out from the cottage, and Pippa was curious to see what was going on inside. She approached the door and peered in. The floor was covered by tarpaulin, and then two figures emerged from the lounge, carrying a rolled up rug. They saw Pippa and scowled at her. She quickly moved out of the way, not wishing to impede their way to the van, and she thought then that she had better leave. However, as she turned on her heels someone called out to her.

"Can I help you?" his voice was rough, and his expression was sour. He was a stocky man with a stained white T shirt that was too small for him. His jeans were black, and a hard hat perched on his head.

"Sorry, no, it's just… I used to live here and I was curious about the work being done," Pippa said, wearing her politest smile. It did not seem to have any effect on the man, however.

"Oh right, well, keep out of the way and make sure he doesn't wander around," the foreman said, gesturing to Jasper. "Did you leave something here?"

"No, I was just passing and thought I'd have a look."

"Right," the foreman stared at her with an icy look. "Well, I have a lot of things to be getting on with so it's probably for the best if you move on. I can't really be having visitors here in case something happens, you know, it's the insurance."

"Of course," Pippa said, but before she left she realized that she too was curious about the man who had bought the house. "Is the owner here? I thought I might have a quick word with him if it's possible."

The foreman shook his head and muttered something under his breath. "I don't know, and I don't have time for idle conversation. I'm on a strict timetable, so if you don't mind I'll get back to work," he turned his back to her, making it clear that he wasn't going to entertain any notion she had of occupying his time. No doubt he must have thought that she was some meddling local, just like the neighbors. Pippa looked forlornly toward the house as she watched more things being carried out. It seemed as though whoever had bought the cottage was gutting it completely. It would never be the same again.

2

Her journey back to the farm took her along the seafront once again. The waves rushed against the shore, and the spray tinged the air with a cool freshness. Pippa did not walk along the beach this time, however, instead she headed for the pub where Braw Ben stood behind the bar as always, smiling widely as she entered. He was wiping down the bar, but stopped as he tossed a treat to Jasper, who took his customary place by the fire, and then served Pippa her usual drink.

"What's on your mind Pippa? You have that look about you," he said, leaning his brawny arms against the bar.

"What look would that be?"

"The look that says you want to talk about something. It's a look I see a lot of people with in here. I think maybe I should start charging what therapists charge," he said with a grin.

"You're certainly worth every penny," Pippa sighed. "I've just been for a walk down to the cottage. Seeing it the way it is now, it's being changed and it just reminds me that nothing lasts forever."

"It surely doesn't. The only thing we can be sure of in this world is that everything is eventually going to change, that's what my grandad used to tell me and the same thing is still true today. I've stood at this bar and I've seen so many things change since I was a boy. I've seen people come and go, I've seen the seasons flow into each other, and I've seen the shops open up and close down again. It's all a part of history though."

"And you're here, like a guardian watching over it all."

"I wouldn't go that far. I'm just a simple man who knows how to pour a good pint," he said with his disarming smile. "But aye, I've seen a lot happen over the years since I was a wee nipper being taught how to serve the customers. Used to be this place was filled with punters and Dad would load me up with an empty tray. I'd walk around and people would put their empties on it. By the time I got back to the bar I'd be weighed down by it all," he said, which went some way to explaining his broad shoulders and strong muscles.

Pippa glanced around at the empty place. There were only a few souls in the pub now. "Do you ever wish it was like it used to be?"

Braw Ben shrugged. "I mean, the days are longer, but I'm more relaxed than my parents ever were. To be honest I'm glad they passed on before they could see what this place became though. I don't think they would have been pleased. They poured their hearts and their souls into this place, and they might think that they put all that effort in for nothing."

"Do you feel that way?"

"No, I've been born and bred to sit here, and the way I look at it, as long as I've got at least one person in the pub then I'm doing some good. Besides, this place has been in my family for generations. I wouldn't know what else to do with myself. Someone has to carry on the tradition."

Pippa pursed her lips and nodded. "It must be nice, to be surrounded by so much history," she glanced up at some of the framed pictures hanging on the walls, each one depicting a different era of people. "What would you do if you had to sell the pub? It would be hard, wouldn't it, to leave behind all of this family history?"

Braw Ben looked to the side and chewed loudly on a piece of gum. He scratched his head and rubbed his chin. "You know, I haven't really thought about that. I suppose it would be a shame, aye, but as long as I carried them in my heart then I'd be okay with it. That's all you can do really, isn't it? Even buildings crumble, but the soul is an eternal thing. I'm going to carry that with me all the way to heaven. Anyway, life is always about moving forward. You can't spend too long looking at the past because you'll get lost in it. There's a whole world out there that is still filled with all manner of good things, and you shouldn't miss them because you've been too busy looking at something you can't change."

He punctuated his word with a strong nod, and she offered a sweet smile in response. Braw Ben could always be counted on to have some kind of insight, and she knew he was right.

"Now Pippa, is there any mystery you've gotten yourself involved in recently?" he asked, seeking to change the topic.

Pippa shook her head. There hadn't been a mystery since Clive had died. "Everything has been quiet around here for a while," she said.

"Then maybe that's the problem!" he slapped the bar with his hand, startling Pippa. "You should get your teeth stuck into something new. A woman like you isn't made to sit idle. You need to be doing something in the world. Here, it's not like the mysteries that you're used to, but I might have something for you," he proceeded to rummage around the back of the bar before he appeared again, brandishing a credit card. He placed the sleek black card onto the counter. "You can try and track down the owner of this card if you like. He was in here last night, acting like a loudmouth. He wanted the most expensive bottle of whiskey and then when I showed him what I had he sneered at me as though it wasn't good enough. Well, I tried calling out to him when I realized he had left his card on the counter, but he just waltzed out as though it wasn't a problem for him. Figured he would be back today to pick it up, but he hasn't appeared."

Pippa put her finger on the credit card and then pulled it toward her. "I guess I don't have anything better to do," she said. Even though a mystery had not presented itself, she wasn't sure if she would be able to throw herself into one after what had happened the last time. It had been a flurry of crime, from two murders in Leeds, to a scandal at a bingo hall, and then the accidental poisoning of a dog before she realized why Clive was involved in this scheme to get Granddad's treasure. She had had a good break now, but she wasn't sure if the mysteries were a positive influence in her life. She had thought that she was doing good by bringing these people to justice, but what kind of a toll was it taking on her? After what had happened with Clive she wasn't sure if she could endure anymore, but she supposed finding the owner of a credit card wasn't going to lead her into too much trouble.

Before she pursued the matter she had another stop to make, and that was to the small café that Callie ran. Pippa had been spending a lot of time with Callie in recent months as the wedding plans continued apace and the two of them had deepened their friendship. Pippa knocked on the door, seeing that Callie was just cleaning up for the night. Callie unlocked the door and set out two chairs for them to sit down on. She made some tea and gave Jasper a little treat. The evening was still light outside, making the daytime seem perennial. Pippa didn't mind this at all, for the longer she could stave off the night the better, in her opinion.

"... and I have dress fitting soon. You'll be able to come, won't you?" Callie asked. She had to then nudge Pippa, as Pippa had become distracted, falling prey to the dark thoughts that lurked like predators in her mind.

"Sorry Callie, yes, of course I'll be there. Just tell me the time and place."

Callie bowed her head and spoke in a quiet voice. "You know you don't have to be my maid of honor if it's too much for you."

Pippa felt abashed. She leaned forward and placed her hand on Callie's knee. "Of course I want to. I'm sorry Callie, it's just that sometimes my mind tends to run away with itself. Being your maid of honor is one of the few things that's keeping me going. I'm really looking forward to it and I wouldn't change it for the world," Pippa said. Callie brightened at this and the smile returned to her face.

"Good, I just want to make sure that everything goes well. I'm getting overwhelmed because everything is a big decision and I just want it to be perfect."

Part of Pippa's job as a maid of honor was to ensure that Callie did not allow herself to get caught up in the occasion. "It's going to be great Callie, and as long as you're sure about Tim then everything will be fine. You are sure about him, aren't you?" Pippa asked with arched eyebrows, just wanting to make sure that Callie hadn't gotten herself into a tricky situation. But Callie's smile stretched even wider and her eyes sparkled with love.

"Oh I am. He's just the most wonderful man. He never has a bad thing to say about anyone and he works so hard, and he's always trying his best to make me feel special."

"So you're not worried about his clumsiness?"

Callie laughed. "I find it endearing really, and frankly there are a lot worse things he can be. I keep telling him that he should stop being a handyman, but he says he wouldn't know how to be anything else so what can I do?" she held up her hands in a helpless gesture. "It does mean that sometimes I worry more than I should, like now. I haven't heard from him all day and it makes me wonder if he's gotten into some scrape. He's probably lost his phone, but usually he comes by the café to tell me that something happened," Callie went quiet and Pippa could tell that she was trying to not be worried.

"Where was he last?" she asked.

"He said he was going for a walk along the beach this morning."

"So he's been gone the entire day?" Pippa asked with arched eyebrows. Callie nodded. "Why didn't you say anything Callie? I'll go and look for him. You stay here in case he comes by. I'm sure he's safe, but with Tim you never know."

Callie offered a weak smile as Pippa and Jasper were spurred into action.

3

Pippa muttered under her breath as she strode toward the beach, wondering how on earth Tim could get into another scrape when he was about to be married. It wasn't fair to Callie to keep having to cope with incidents like this, and Pippa hoped that she would be able to find Tim in order to give him a good scolding. She found herself standing in the middle of the beach. To her right the beach stretched out and melted into a rising cliff, while the ground became narrower and lower to her left. Everything else was the sea, stretching out into infinity, the murky blue that shifted and danced melted into the horizon, creating a sense that they were stitched together like some tapestry. Pippa wondered where Tim could have gotten to. The worst case scenario was that he had been washed out to sea, but she didn't want to think about that because it would mean that there was no chance of a happy ending, and Callie certainly didn't deserve that. If there was anyone who needed to feel the warm joy of bliss then it was Callie. She didn't have a mean bone in her body, and there was no cause for fate to punish her like this.

So Pippa then thought about where Tim might have gone. Her gaze fell on a path toward the narrow part of the land, a path that was hidden when the tide came in. She checked her watch. She still had a bit of time before it was covered, but she was going to have to hurry. With Jasper by her side, she marched across and made her way across the uneven rocks. The spray from the water was getting ever nearer and made the rocks slick. She held onto the other rocks for dear life, afraid that if she fell then the current would carry her out to sea and there would be no escape.

When she almost slipped, she thought that this was reckless, especially when she had no idea if Tim was actually waiting for her at the end. After all, how far was she going to follow the path before she was too far from land? Jasper looked wary as well, and did not seem to trust the rocks. Pippa huffed, annoyed at Tim for getting himself into this kind of situation. But just as she was about to return to the beach and try another method of searching for him, she saw a light winking at her from one of the small caves. At first she blinked, wondering if it was just a trick of the light, but there was definitely something reflecting the sunlight, winking at her. She looked back to the beach, and knew that she wouldn't have been able to see it from any other angle other than where she was currently standing, and just in case it was Tim she could not afford to turn away.

"Alright Jasper, wait there. I'll be back soon," she said. Jasper whimpered a little as he settled down, staring at her. It was rare for Pippa to be alone and as she ventured onto the slick rocks she suddenly felt vulnerable. If she was swept away to the ocean that would be it, an unceremonious end to her life. She walked carefully and kept as close to the bluff as possible, holding her hand out to make sure that she could grab the rocks in case she fell. Although she moved slowly, the winking light wasn't actually too far from her position, although the water continued to lap toward her feet, as though it was coaxing her to plunge into the sea.

Pippa grit her teeth and continued on her path, reaching the mouth of the small cave. Inside she saw Tim sitting there, stretching out to hold his phone to the light, turning it from left to right. As soon as he saw Pippa he gasped with relief and let out a triumphant noise.

"Pippa! Is it really you?" he cried, suggesting that he might have suspected he was afraid of falling into delusion.

"Yes Tim, it's me. What are you doing out here?" she asked, trying and failing to keep the scolding tone out of her voice.

Before he could answer, however, she scanned the cave and noticed that Tim wasn't alone. Pressed against the far wall was a vague outline she had to strain to see, but when she did she saw that it was a dead body. Tim was with a corpse again. Pippa groaned and her shoulders slumped. "Oh Tim, what's happened now?" she asked.

"Tim glanced across and held up his hands. "I have nothing to do with it! He was here when I got here."

"And how did you get here in the first place?" Pippa put her hands on her hips as she moved her gaze between Tim and the corpse.

"Well, I was walking along the beach trying to think of what to say in my speech. I want to make sure that Callie knows how much she means to me and how lucky I am, but I can't seem to think of the right words. I thought the sea air would do me good. I found myself out here and when I looked back, well, the sea kept looking as though it was going to take me back. I don't know how I managed to make it this far really," he offered a small smile. Pippa assumed that he must have been so lost in thought he hadn't allowed his clumsy nature to take effect. Once he was actually cognizant of the task ahead he became unsteady.

"So you just decided to stay here?"

"Well, to get my balance yes. I was hoping that the tide would go out and that it would be easier to walk back. I checked my phone because I wanted to call Callie, but then it ran out of battery and then I saw this poor chap here."

Pippa looked at the corpse. It was dressed in a suit, its face was pale, its hair flecked wet by the spray of water that cascaded into the cave. His arms were ramrod straight and his eyes were open and his face registered shock. It was difficult to tell much in the way of detail about the body because of the darkness. It seemed as though Pippa did indeed have a mystery to solve now.

"The only thing I could think to do was try and get someone's attention by reflecting the sunlight off my phone. I'm so very glad you came to find me."

"You could have tried walking back Tim. I know it seems daunting, but it's really not very far."

Tim looked admonished. "Well, about that…" he trailed away and then looked down at his foot. Pippa followed his gaze and saw that it had become stuck in a hole. Pippa sighed and rubbed her temples.

"I really don't know how you manage to keep getting yourself involved in things like this Tim."

"Me neither," he said forlornly, "it seemed to appear from nowhere. Before I could do anything about it my foot was stuck. I can't seem to twist it right to get it free. I've been stuck here all day. I was afraid I was going to have to spend the night here."

"Well it's a good thing that's not going to happen. I'll get you free," Pippa said, thinking that this was not the kind of thing she had signed up for when it came to maid of honor duties, but she wasn't going to let Callie's groom be lost in some cave.

Pippa got to her knees and felt around the hole, trying to get a good grip on Tim's foot. As she did so, she glanced across at the man.

"Any idea who he is?"

Tim shook his head. "I didn't want to disturb the body in case it was important. I don't recognize him though. Do you think he could have washed up from the sea?"

"I think he would be a little wetter if that was the case," Pippa said. She yanked with great effort, and then twisted, and then pulled Tim's foot free. He yelped with pain and gingerly stretched out his foot, getting used to the blood flowing through it again. He winced and gasped as he moved it from side to side, and while he recovered Pippa crawled into the cave to examine the body a little more closely. The man looked to be in his forties, or perhaps fifties. His suit was smart, and his hair had thinned. She glanced back out of the cave. It would have been difficult for anyone to bring a body here during the day without anyone else seeing it, but at night it would have been even harder, what with the current. She furrowed her brow, wondering how this man had gotten here. She then wondered if he had walked here, like Tim, and had died of starvation. That theory was pushed away as she rummaged around his body to find his wallet, also finding a stab wound.

There was no doubt about it, this man had been murdered.

She pocketed the wallet and helped Tim to his feet.

"We need to get back to town so I can tell Arthur about this. There could be another murderer on the loose."

"Another one? Good grief!" Tim bemoaned.

Pippa helped Tim limp out of the cave and then steadied him as he made his way back. The water teased them, and Pippa had to reassure Tim that nothing bad was going to happen to him as long as he just kept moving forward. When they eventually returned to the beach Jasper was waiting for them.

"Promise me you'll be more careful in the future. You mean a lot to Callie and I want the two of you to have a long and happy life with each other. She's not ready to become a widow just yet. Next time you find yourself being lost in thought just take a moment to look at your surroundings and you might find that it's going to be safer, to go to the church whenever you have something to ponder. The Reverend won't let anything bad happen to you," Pippa said. Tim looked embarrassed, but took her advice in the spirit that it was intended. Pippa then led him back to the café and told Callie that she found something that had been lost. Callie took one look at Tim's disheveled clothes and pulled him in for a hug, set him in a chair, and then poured him a cup of tea before she went to make him some food. It was cute to see them together like this, and adorable to see Callie dote on Tim. As Jack had said previously, some people in this world need to be looked after, and some people needed to look after others.

Pippa still hadn't quite worked out which category she fit into yet.

But for now she had other things to work about, because there was a murder afoot.

4

Pippa had only popped into the police station for social visits over the past few months as she enjoyed Arthur's company and quite missed working cases with him. Things in Burlybottom on Sea had been quiet, and nothing like this had happened. She had begun to wonder if her spate of solving mysteries had come to an end, but it appeared as though her skills would be needed again. Perhaps Braw Ben was right, and what she really needed was to get her teeth into a grisly crime.

"Pippa! What a pleasant delight. I was just going to call it a night and return home, but I suppose I can wait here for a cup of tea if you'd like to join me?" Arthur said, smiling delightedly. Jasper walked up to him and nuzzled his head against Arthur's legs.

"We're definitely going to need one, I just found something disturbing," she said, and proceeded to tell

Arthur about the body in the cave. Arthur sank to his chair and stroked his chin.

"Oh right, well that does sound troublesome. And a stab wound you say?"

"That's what it looks like to me. Obviously I didn't have a chance to have a long examination. I wanted to get back before the tide came in. I just hope it leaves the body there."

"It should. The tide doesn't tend to reach into those caves. It just makes it impossible for people to get there at night."

"It can't have been impossible for whoever left the body there. I can't imagine they would have been able to get the corpse there in daylight, and if they walked there surely someone would have seen that only one person returned?"

"You'd be surprised at what people can miss. Not everyone is as observant as you or I," Arthur said, leaning back in his chair. "Is there anything else you can tell me?"

"Well, I got this," Pippa pulled out the wallet and placed it on the desk in front of Arthur.

"I suppose we should see what's in here then," he proceeded to open the black leather wallet. There were a few notes of cash as well as some coins, membership cards, a train ticket, and debit and credit cards. Pippa glimpsed a photo of the man on one of the membership cards. It was definitely the same man in the cave. "Well, it seems this chap's name is Marcus Philby," Arthur said.

Pippa creased her brow a little. The name seemed familiar, but from where? She reached into her pocket again and pulled out the card that Braw Ben had given her. She looked at the name that was printed on the black card in studded silver letters; Steven Philby. She passed the card to Arthur, telling him that it had been left in Braw Ben's pub the previous night.

"Well, what are the chances that two men with the same name are in the same town on the same night."

"And one of them ends up dead," Pippa said, arching her eyebrows. It certainly seemed suspicious, and she could not believe that there wasn't a connection between the two men. At the very least Steven might be able to give them some insight into who exactly Marcus was, and why he was in Burlybottom on Sea.

Unfortunately they did not have anything other than the names to go on. Marcus' address was listed as somewhere in London, so it seemed that they were visitors. The only lead this gave them was that they might be staying in a hotel. She and Arthur began telephoning the local guest houses to ask if they had any guests by this name. They made slow progress at first, and Arthur expressed frustration that it was going to take all night to phone every hotel in the area. Pippa leaned back and thought about the way Braw Ben had described Steven's behavior. He said Steven had wanted the most expensive bottle of whiskey, and clearly by the amount of cards in Marcus' wallet he was an affluent man. It seemed logical to assume that they enjoyed the finer things in life and so that could narrow Pippa and Arthur's search to the more high end hotels in the area. They started with the most expensive and worked their way down from there, but as it turned out they didn't have to work their way down at all. The receptionist told them that yes, there was a guest by the name of Steven Philby staying with them.

Pippa and Arthur left the police station immediately.

Pippa found that it was far easier to get past the receptionist when she had a policeman by her side, unlike in London when she had had the police called on her, in her search for Clive. The hotel was set in the countryside away from the rest of the world, boasting high class service, a spa, and any other luxury treatment someone could think of. The ambience of the place was gentle and serene, although this was disrupted by Arthur and Pippa marching through the halls. Jasper was in between them both.

"Even though I'm not happy that someone has died, it's nice to be working with you again Pippa. I have missed this."

"Me too," Pippa admitted. "Ben told me that it might have been something missing from my life over the past few months. I haven't been feeling quite right."

"Well, you're not going to after what happened to you. But you're strong and you're capable of moving on. I'm just glad you haven't disappeared into yourself. That's the worst thing that can happen. People need to keep busy and need to keep thinking about the way that life moves forward, and you've done exactly that. But you know that if you ever need anything then you can always come and talk to me."

"I appreciate that Arthur," Pippa said. The police constable had been a staunch friend since he had arrived in Burlybottom on Sea, and Pippa valued their relationship. Given their age difference he was something of a father figure to her, filling a hole in her life that had been present for a long time. It was nice to know that he was there to support her even when times were tough.

But she did not have much time to dwell on that at the present moment, not when they were hot on the heels of a potential murderer. They reached Steven's room and rapped on the door loudly. Arthur barked that he was the police, and soon enough the door swung open. Standing before them was a man dressed in a robe. His hair was tousled, there were shadows under his eyes, and stubble lined his chin. The stench of alcohol permeated the room, and as Pippa peered beyond him she could see that the minibar had been raided, its contents drained and empty, littered on the floor like bottles that had washed up onto shore.

"What do you want?" he sneered, leaning against the frame of the door. Pippa estimated that he was in his twenties, although the state of him made him look older.

"Are you Steven Philby?"

"Who wants to know?"

Arthur sighed with frustration and flashed his badge again.

"Yes that's me," Steven said.

"Do you know a Marcus Philby?"

"That's my Dad," he said, and belched as the words came out.

"When was the last time you saw your father?" Arthur asked.

Steven shrugged. "Yesterday morning I suppose."

"I see. Well I think you should get yourself cleaned up because you're going to need to come to the station with us. I'm sorry to inform you that your father is dead."

Steven staggered back and then turned away from them. He disappeared into the bathroom and shut the door. Pippa and Arthur glanced at each other, wondering if this was the sign of a guilty conscience or not. In time Steven appeared. He had splashed water over his face and had changed his clothes. He wore a surly look on his face as he walked past them.

"Let's get this over with," he said.

They were back at the station. Arthur had brewed Steven some coffee in the hope that it would sober him up. Steven was slumped in a chair, his expression unchanged since the hotel.

"So what do you want to know?" Steven asked as Arthur and Pippa came in. Jasper sat by Pippa's feet.

"First of all I'd like to know a little bit about you. What do you do?" Arthur asked.

"I'm a banker. I live in London."

"And what are you doing here?" Arthur asked.

"No comment," Steven replied after a long pause. Arthur and Pippa shared a glance. This was clearly not going to be as easy as they might have thought. At this juncture Pippa didn't think that Steven was responsible for Marcus' death because she assumed he would have fled the scene of the crime. There may have been another reason for him sticking around though, and the only way to tell would be through questioning.

"You do realize that this night is going to be very long for you if you don't cooperate with our questions. All we're looking for at the moment is information about your father and if we know why he was here then we might be able to find his killer. Surely you can't object to us trying to find that information, unless you have a reason to hide it from us?" Arthur asked.

Unease rippled across Steven's face. He shifted in his seat and tapped his fingers on the surface of the table.

"If you must know I came here to stop him from moving here. I don't understand why he'd want to trade the city for this place," he wore a look of disdain. Pippa and Arthur both tried to not take it personally, but Steven did not care that he was insulting their home. "He's moving into some dump of a cottage but he has to renovate it first. Whoever owned it before him let it get rundown. I've never seen a place in such a state. I can't understand why he wanted to give London up, so I thought I'd come here to speak some sense into him," he said.

Since there were not many cottages being renovated in Burlybottom on Sea, it was not a difficult leap of logic to learn that he was talking about Pippa's former home, and indeed this was confirmed after providing a quick description of the place. So Marcus was the man who had bought the cottage, and now he was dead.

Was that place cursed?

"I was the one who used to live there," Pippa said icily. Steven did not offer anything in the way of an apology, he just waved his hand in the air, so she decided to get creative. "So it seems clear that you did not want him to move. Perhaps you became agitated when he was adamant that this is where he wanted to live. You couldn't understand, so you became irate and annoyed, and this boiled over into anger, or was it because he did give you a reason? A reason you didn't like? Maybe you were the one who killed him. Did you feel betrayed that he left you?"

Her words were quick and she had to admit a sense of satisfaction that cascaded through her as she spoke. However, this feeling was fleeting and cut short when he crossed his arms and formed a stony expression. "I'm not going to say anything without my lawyer. I want a phone call now," he said.

"I'm sorry for blowing that. I thought if I pushed him he might have slipped up," Pippa said. "I guess I'm a little out of practice."

"Don't worry about it. On another person that might have worked. He's cannier than I initially gave him credit for. We'll see what this lawyer has to say though. Look, I have some paperwork to file and I need to arrange for a team to bring the body onto land. Why don't you go and get some rest. I doubt anything else is going to be done tonight," Arthur said.

Pippa nodded, although she knew that she would not be able to sleep. She had the thrill of a mystery coursing through her mind and her soul again, and oh she had missed it. She was on the trail of injustice again, and she couldn't wait to get to the sweet core of the puzzle and learn the truth.

5

Since Pippa couldn't sleep, she did not return to the farm just yet as she knew that in order to solve this mystery she was going to need some more information, and where else to turn but the cottage? Now that she knew Marcus was the one who bought it she assumed that there would be some information there, if she could get inside. As she arrived, however, she was dismayed to see the foreman there, loading up the van for the night.

"Back again? He still isn't here. I think if you want to see him then you can always leave a message with me," the foreman said, speaking in a frustrated tone.

"Actually I don't think that will be necessary, and I'm not sure you have to be worried about your deadline any longer. I'm afraid to tell you that the man who owned this cottage is dead."

The foreman looked aghast and arched his eyebrows. "And how do you know that? Are you putting me on?"

"I work with the police here," Pippa said. "So now I'd like to know when you last saw the victim."

The foreman muttered something under his breath and his face paled. He crossed his arms and dug his hands deep under his arm pits. For a moment she was afraid that he was going to refuse to speak to her without a lawyer, but he wasn't as sly as Steven.

"I saw him yesterday I think, although only briefly. He was on the phone."

"And what was your relationship with him like?"

The foreman shrugged. "It was okay I guess. Didn't speak to him much. He told us what he wanted and then let us get on with the job. That's the kind of client I like. He did seem distracted a lot though, like he was always staring into space. I didn't speak with him much. We're from different worlds, him and I. He seemed to have a lot of business to take care of. He was always on the phone. The likes of us don't usually mix together."

"I see, and what works are being carried out on the house?"

The foreman, who by now had introduced himself as Harry, glanced at the cottage. "Simple renovation work mostly. It's not a tough job, he just wants the place updated. New floors, new walls, better glazing on the windows, the only thing he was adamant about was that he wanted one of the bedrooms finished first. Other than that he just let us get on with the job and trusted us to get it done. Like I said, he's the kind of client I like. He didn't interfere and he didn't try and do our jobs for us."

Pippa wondered if the second bedroom was for the son as a guest room, although that didn't quite seem to fit with how the dynamic of the relationship had been described to her by Steven.

"I see, well, I'll probably need to get in touch with you and the other workers as well, and anyone else who has been on the site. At the moment I'm not able to rule out anyone I'm afraid, so please tell your men to not leave the area for the time being."

"I can tell you for sure that none of my men would have done anything to him. They all value their jobs more than that," Harry said indignantly.

Pippa smiled. "Of course, but we must go through the proper procedure," she replied, thinking that there could always be a motive for murder lurking unseen in the background, beyond the field of vision. Until she spoke to these men for herself she would not be able to rule them out as suspects. Perhaps things weren't as cordial with all of the workers as Harry claimed. Perhaps Marcus was the type of man to have his temper flare, and if he caught the wrong man at the wrong time there was no telling what could have happened.

Pippa watched the white van drive away, and as it did so something caught her eye or, rather, someone. Down the other side of the road, peering out from a thicket of trees was a woman with white blonde hair. She was staring straight at the cottage. Pippa strode off in that direction, trying to wave the woman down, but by the time she reached the thicket of trees the woman had disappeared. Pippa frowned, wondering if this new element was something to do with the case at all, or was something else entirely.

Who was Marcus Philby, and what kind of life did he lead?

As she walked back she avoided speaking to Mindy and Martha as she did not want to reveal to them yet that a murder had taken place. They peered out of the window toward her though, and she pretended not to see.

By the time she returned to the barn it was late at night. The long hours of the day had finally given way and now the stars were aglow above. She noticed that Jack's light was on in his bedroom, but she thought it was too late to disturb him. The last thing he needed was to think about his idyllic corner of the world being tainted by death and murder yet again. Instead, she went to bed with Jasper laying nearby in his bed, and pulled the blankets right up to her neck. Her mind turned with the fragments of the case that she had so far, trying to fit them together and solve the puzzle even though she did not have all of the pieces yet. However, this was a welcome distraction as for once it meant she was not thinking about Clive when she fell asleep. It seemed as though Ben had been right, all she needed was a good mystery to sink her teeth into.

6

P ippa was awoken first thing in the morning by her phone's shrill ring. It was a different noise than the alarm, and one that sent Jasper yapping away. Pippa awoke with a start, flinging the blankets off her as she picked up the phone and held it to her ear.

"I think you had better get down here. The lawyer has arrived, and she's a vicious one," Arthur said in a hushed voice. At first Pippa worried she had slept in late, but when she checked the time it was early in the morning. The lawyer must have driven all through the night to make it down here. Either she was dedicated to her clients, or Steven was paying her handsomely. Perhaps there was an element of both. Pippa quickly got ready for the day and then made her way to the police station.

When she arrived, she saw Steven's lawyer sitting beside him. The woman had a prominent jaw, long dark hair, and a stern expression. In fact there was something familiar about her, which Pippa would soon learn was because this woman was, in fact, Steven's mother, Kim Philby, although she went by her maiden name of Swinell.

"Isn't this a conflict of interest given your relationship to Steven and to Marcus?" Pippa asked. It was the first question that popped into her mind when she became aware of the nature of their relationship.

Kim sighed and flicked away a strand of hair. "I am here only to represent my son. My husband is not my husband any longer and I have nothing more to say about him. I am simply here to protect my son's –" she caught herself, "my *client's* innocence. I am the best lawyer he could hope for and all I'm going to do is make sure that he has the best defense. My husband and I are waiting for a divorce."

"What happened?" Pippa asked casually.

Kim seemed to consider whether she should answer or not, but her bitterness eventually consumed her. Pippa had learned that most people were eager to take any opportunity to take a dig at someone who had hurt them.

"Like so many other men he couldn't keep his hands to himself." Each one of Kim's words were perfectly formed, her tongue was as sharp as a sword. Pippa did not know much about the victim, but he must have known the risk of crossing such a formidable woman. Steven slumped in the chair, trying to disappear. Pippa's gaze studied him. Was this a man who had been caught in the crossfire

47

between his parents? Did he resent his father for cheating on his mother, or had he tried to be the peacemaker between the two of them? Unfortunately Pippa was not going to be able to find out because, thanks to Kim, Steven's lips were fastened shut with red tape. It was going to take more than an earnest heart to pry them open.

"Now, I'm going to take Steven out of this awful place because the only thing linking him to the crime is that he is related to the victim. There is no physical evidence, no witness statements, nothing to suggest he had anything to do with it aside from his blood, and that is not a good enough reason to keep him in this sorry excuse for a police station. Steven, get up and let's go," she said this sternly and easily, and Pippa could well imagine she had spent her life barking these orders like a general to Steven. And with the way Steven rose as though pulled up by strings, he seemed well versed in obeying her orders as well.

Kim walked out with Steven. Arthur called out, reminding her that Steven had to remain in the vicinity of the crime, because if he took flight it might well seem like an admission of guilt. Kim grunted in reply.

"What a thoroughly unpleasant woman," Arthur sighed as he shook his head."

"I suppose one could admire her protective attitude toward her son."

"That's if you believe she's doing it purely out of the kindness of her heart. She clearly knows more than she's letting on. They both do. And they're going to hide it from us."

"Do you think one of them might have killed Marcus?"

Arthur breathed out of his nose. The air tickled his mustache. "I don't like making presumptions Pippa, but there is clearly a lot of resentment in the family. If Steven was drinking then he might have done something rash."

"Or perhaps he was drinking because he had done something rash," Pippa wondered aloud. Arthur raised his eyebrows and sighed again.

"Well, either way she is dedicated to her profession, or her son. She made it here from London in record time."

Despite the disappointment of having their prime, and only, suspect taken out of custody, there was a break in the case as the body was able to be collected from the cave. It took a team of men rowing out to the cave to pull the body into a boat, which then returned to the beach. They then carried the body up the beach into a van. Word had spread among the inhabitants of the seaside town, and given that this was such an unusual occurrence a crowd had gathered. People were rising on their tiptoes and peering toward the cave in the hope that they might catch a glimpse of the dead body. Pippa thought it was entirely morbid, and wondered why people were so fascinated with the concept of death. She had to believe that these people had better things to do with their lives.

Some of them were even eating fish and chips.

Arthur was there to ensure that a path was cleared as the corpse was carried up to land. People whispered and muttered amongst themselves. Pippa supposed that most of them would never see a dead body. Her mind flashed back to the moment she had peered off the top of St. Paul's Cathedral and looked down to see the silent men, all that they were, having been stripped from them by the impact of crashing to the ground. Pippa's throat tightened and she took a deep breath, feeling all the emotions shuddering through her. She turned, trying to put the thought out of her mind, and faced the street instead of the beach.

That's when she saw the woman again. She was certain that it was the same woman she had seen outside the cottage. Pippa's brow crinkled and before she knew it she was striding through the crowd, making her way up from the sandy beach to the cold concrete. The woman's gaze was focused on the beach, but when she saw Pippa coming toward her she turned immediately and disappeared. By the time Pippa had reached the street it was too late, there was no trace of the woman. Jasper caught the scent, but he followed it into thick bramble and Pippa looked back, torn between chasing after this woman or returning to see what a closer examination of the body could reveal. Given that this woman might have had nothing to do with it, and that it might take some time for Pippa to find her, Pippa decided to turn back.

Arthur was there in the back of the medical van, while people had formed a throng nearby. As Pippa returned she could hear Arthur periodically yelling at them to stay back. Pippa made her way through and looked at the pale, damp body. Now that she had proper light to aid her vision she could see the body properly. The wound was a dark shadow on his clothes. An examiner was there and Arthur asked him for a quick deduction, although a full analysis would arrive later. Pippa and Arthur could not wait though; they needed a break in the case.

The medical examiner leaned over the body. "It's clearly a stab wound. Given the depth of the wound I would say that the impact came from a short distance. I will need more time with the body before I come to any certain conclusions, but from what I can see here it looks as though the weapon would be something sharp, long, and narrow."

"Like a screwdriver?" Pippa asked absently. The medical examiner considered the suggestion for a moment and then nodded. Perhaps they had been off base with their assumption that Steven had anything to do with it at all. After all, there was a house filled with construction workers who could also be suspects.

7

This time Arthur joined Pippa in returning to the cottage. He flashed his identification as soon as he arrived, bringing the foreman to heel, for Pippa had forewarned him that Harry could be difficult.

"I thought we had already dealt with this?" Harry put his hands on his hips.

"I see that you're carrying on with the work," Pippa said. The cottage was still busy with people moving around like ants.

"As long as we're getting paid for it, yeah. I'll do the job until I'm told differently," Harry said.

"Well we need to ask you a few questions about your relationship with the deceased," Arthur said.

Harry pressed his lips together and when he spoke Pippa

could tell that he was making a conscious effort to keep his tone calm.

"I already told you that I didn't have any relationship with him other than a professional one. He was the one who wanted the work done and he paid us. That's as far as it went."

"So neither you nor one of your men had any disagreements with him? You never saw any sign of a dispute or an argument?"

Harry glanced back inside the house and his head dropped forward, seemingly conflicted. He glanced at Arthur's badge. If he was torn between loyalty to his crew and obedience to the law, then it was the obedience that won. He sidled closer to Arthur and Pippa, lowering his voice.

"Look, I can vouch for all the men here. We've been working together for a long time and I wouldn't have any of them here if I couldn't trust them. I spend more time with them than I do my own wife, so I'm not going to have anyone here who gives me a bad a vibe. Frankly I think you're looking in the wrong place if you're looking here for a killer."

"I understand that Harry," Arthur said, "but unfortunately we can't just take your word for it. Now, did any of them have any disagreement with Marcus?"

Harry's eyes closed for a moment and he shook his head. "You'll want to speak to Phil. He'll be around the back, working on the door."

"What happened between them?" Pippa asked.

"I don't really know the details. Marcus could be... particular in what he wanted. I saw Phil storm away the other day after Marcus had been walking through the house. He didn't come to me with any complaints, so I didn't think it was a big deal."

"Do the men often come to you with their complaints?" Arthur asked.

"I'm the foreman," Harry said, as though that explained everything. "If they have a problem then it's my job to sort it out with the client. They don't need to get involved with them. They all know this, so if Phil had a serious problem then he would have come to me."

"Or he would have kept things quiet because he didn't want to involve you," Pippa said. Harry glared at her and curled his lips.

"I've told you everything I know. It's up to you to make that judgment about Phil now," Harry then walked away. Pippa and Arthur glanced toward each other.

"You think he's telling the truth?" she asked.

"I think he's right when he says that he knows these men better than anyone else. But I also know that they're a close knit group, and sometimes in these situations they circle the wagons and try to protect their own. We need to speak to Phil and see what he has to say.

Pippa and Arthur moved to the back of the cottage. Despite Harry's proud assurance that they were still working, many of the men were taking a break. As Pippa moved around the cottage she peered inside the windows, and was shocked at how much it had changed. The kitchen, for example, was being completely remade. In the garden there was a skip that was filled with all the old cabinets and stove, everything being completely gutted for new things. She knew that change was an important and necessary part of life, but she would have preferred it if, in this instance, it had happened away from her view.

Phil was a man with ginger hair. He was stocky and short. At the present moment he was standing on a ladder, reaching to the top of the doorway and working on the frame. The door had been unhinged and cast into the skip, leaving a gaping hole into the kitchen. Inside there were plastic sheets draped over the floor, and new cabinets waiting to be fastened. These cabinets were a lighter shade of wood than what had been there before, and there was even a new countertop in the middle of the room.

"Are you Phil?" Arthur asked. Phil glanced down and saw the police identification.

"Harry mentioned you were asking around. I suppose you're here to ask me about Marcus? Truth is I didn't know him that well," Phil said, and turned to go back to work. He assumed that they were just here to ask routine questions, but that wasn't the case at all.

"I'm afraid that it's a little more serious than that. Is it true that you and Marcus had an argument the day he died?" Arthur asked. Phil hesitated completely. "I think you should descend the ladder."

Phil hung his head and paused for a moment. He descended the ladder rung by rung, his frustration evident in every step. When he had reached the ground he dusted his hands. He was shorter than Pippa had expected. His face was dusted with freckles, as were his arms.

"Are you arresting me?" Phil asked.

"Should I?" Arthur replied.

"Well I don't know how these things work."

"We're just here to ask you a few questions," Pippa said gently. Phil moved away from the door and sat down on a chair. Three chairs had been arranged near the skip, which was evidently a rest area for the workers. He grabbed a bottle of water and drank half the bottle.

"Shoot," he said.

"Well, we'd like you to tell us if you did have an argument with Marcus," Arthur repeated.

"Yes, I did. But I didn't kill him," Phil said.

"What did you argue about?" Pippa asked, taking note of Phil's body language. He leaned forward and rested his arms on his thighs. His hands were clasped together, but as soon as he started speaking they were split apart and waved around the air.

"Just stupid things. Look, some clients are happy for you to get on with the job, and others like to interfere. I get it, it's his house and he deserves to have things the way he wants them. But I was in a bit of a bad mood and wasn't in the mood to hear about how he wanted the sockets two inches this way or two inches that way, or how the door is just the wrong shade of color. I didn't really see how these things were going to make a difference. I doubt he would even notice them. It's like he just wanted to meddle for the sake of meddling. Anyway, I ended up muttering under my breath, which I know I shouldn't have done, and he heard me. He turned around and starts telling me that he's paying a top rate for our services and so if he ever has any problems then he wants to know that they're going to be sorted out. And then he said that he could go and talk to Harry if he had a problem with me and I'd be looking for work. Well, needless to say this got me riled up, but Harry always tells us that we don't have to deal with the client, he does. I could have knocked him out, but I've got people who depend on me, so I swallowed my pride and I called that I was taking a break and I waited until he was gone."

"That sounds like a rational way to handle the situation," Arthur said.

Phil straightened with pride. "I learned that in anger management."

"So what happened after this then? You never saw Marcus again?" Pippa continued the questioning.

Phil shook his head. "I cooled down. By the time I came back Marcus had gone elsewhere in the house. I had enough time to think about it and so I didn't think it was worth mentioning to Harry. This job is good for a lot of us and I didn't want to cause any friction between Marcus and the crew. I told myself that I was just stressed because of what had been happening at home, and I needed to take myself out of the situation. I certainly didn't want to kill him."

Pippa and Arthur glanced at each other.

"While that all makes sense, we do have a piece of evidence to suggest that he was killed by a tool on this building site," Arthur said.

Phil scrunched up his face with indignation. "Well that doesn't mean anything. We leave them here overnight. Anyone could come in and use them."

Pippa tilted her head. "Isn't that dangerous? Aren't you worried about people stealing them?"

"Not my problem. Marcus sorted all that out with Harry. He paid for extra insurance I think, because if the tools are left here it means we can get on with the job more quickly. We don't need to waste time setting everything up and packing it away each day. I guess he figured that in this part of the world there aren't many people who are looking to steal things. It's quiet around here."

"That's a common misconception," Arthur said. If things truly were quiet then there wouldn't have been a need for his presence. "Thank you for your time though Phil. It has been most illuminating."

They asked around to see if anyone else had had any fractious interactions with Marcus, but it seemed as though Phil was the only one. They all agreed that there were moments when Marcus could be particular, but it had never bothered them that much. This left Pippa and Arthur at a bit of a loose end as they walked away from the cottage.

"So it doesn't look like any of these workers were involved," Pippa said.

"Unless they have rallied around each other and are protecting the killer. They are the ones who have been in this cottage more often than others. If the murder weapon was one of their tools then they've had the opportunity to get rid of it, and it's going to be difficult to find the culprit if they're all willing to keep silent."

"They seem to know that they've got a good thing going. Would any of them really want to jeopardize it by killing Marcus? It's not as though it would gain them anything. If anything it would hurt them because it would end the job early and they might not get their full rate of pay. It doesn't seem like any of them would prioritize killing a man over a good payday."

"Indeed, although I would argue that, more often than not, the mind of a killer is an irrational one. Let's try and piece together the events that took place. Marcus bought this cottage, presumably because he and Kim are getting a divorce. He wanted a fresh start, somewhere out in the country away from the city."

"Somewhere his son doesn't like," Pippa interjected. Jasper slalomed in between her legs before settling down.

Arthur nodded. "Marcus moves here anyway. He wants to renovate the place so he hires a building crew. From what little I know of him, Marcus wouldn't be the type to hire a crew that has a bad reputation. He's willing to pay for premium quality, judging by the clothes he was wearing and the materials used in renovating the house. A builder's reputation does not come easily, so we can assume that they have a high standing."

"So Marcus came out here to visit and check up on the renovations. Harry mentioned that he was on the phone a lot."

"Perhaps with business deals, or with Kim and his lawyers to arrange the terms of the divorce."

"Or with Steven."

"Then Steven came down, tries to convince his father to come back, perhaps even to repair the marriage."

"And then Steven is seen later that night getting drunk in Braw Ben's pub."

"And at that point, or earlier, Marcus is killed and his body is taken to the cave in the dark, where Tim finds him the following day."

"There's something we're missing," Pippa curled her fist in frustration.

"Let's take a moment to think about the logistics of the murder. Say that Steven did kill his father, what happens then? He's alone. A dead body is heavy. He knows the construction workers are going to come back the following day. He can't leave the body in the house because the workers are everywhere. They're bound to find it."

"So he panics. He looks outside and he sees the sea."

"But to get out there he's going to have to get a boat."

Arthur pinched the bridge of his nose. "Would he be so stupid to hire one? Even if he was I'm not sure we could get the records. Everything he's done is going to be under lock and key because of Kim. We're going to have to struggle to find some evidence if we're to get anything on him. But the events do line up. He might have gone for a drink at the pub to celebrate his relief because he thought he had just gotten away with murder."

"Maybe he's having another drink now," Pippa said tersely, annoyed that a killer might have gotten away with a crime. "I suppose there's no hope of us finding the murder weapon?"

"It's just a screwdriver. I doubt that the workers would notice if just one of them went missing. They always have spares, and I would assume that Steven, or whoever murdered Marcus, would have had the wherewithal to take the weapon with them."

Pippa nodded sadly. If Steven hadn't murdered Marcus, then who had? They seemed to have ruled out the building crew, but there was one other person Pippa hadn't mentioned to Arthur because she wasn't sure if this person had any significance whatsoever. It was the woman she had seen twice, both times in locations that had relevance to Marcus. Was she just some errant tourist who had found herself a victim of coincidence, or was there something more? Sadly Pippa wasn't sure if she would ever find out, as there was no way to know if she would see this woman again.

It was with a heavy heart that Pippa returned to the farm late at night with lots of thoughts running through her mind. With every piece of information they had, the natural conclusion to draw was that Steven had murdered his father. But they had an incomplete picture, and Pippa did not wish to condemn anyone before she had all the information. However, the suspicion sat too well on Steven's shoulders, and he was not helped by Kim's attempts to steamroll the investigation. Was she just being a protective mother, or was she trying to hide her client's guilt?

Either way, Pippa found it impossible to sleep and so, with the shroud of night completely upon the world with its dark ethereal beauty, she roused herself and walked the path back to the cottage. The world at night was different than in the day. It was quiet, and the whisper of the sea called out to her. The moon was high and full, its reflection glowing upon the wine dark sea, the waves endlessly ebbing and flowing, never ceasing in their eternal dance. It was so quiet and peaceful out here, with all the windows dark as people were lost in dreams. As Pippa and Jasper walked in the middle of the road she felt as though she was the only person in the world. What a sad fate that would be though, to live a life without any friends or family, to have nobody to be a maid of honor for, to have no Reverend to listen to every Sunday, to have no Jack waiting for her at the farm.

The world, and the people within it, could be cruel, but there were so many other people who were worthy of God's love. These murders and other crimes she investigated were sobering, but they also helped her appreciate other people in contrast, as she could see the nobility within them. So she walked a lonely path at night, although her heart was accompanied by all of the generous and lovely people who lived life with her. She was determined to find the truth and bring justice to whomever deserved it, but in order to do that she needed to return to the cottage, rummaging around just in case there were any clues to be found.

8

The vague nature of the case meant that Pippa couldn't even be sure that the cottage was the scene of the crime. Yes, it was assumed that a screwdriver was the murder weapon, but if Steven was the murderer then he might have taken the implement away from the murder scene and perhaps lured Marcus elsewhere, and then the deed could have taken place. Pippa wasn't entirely sure that coming to the cottage was going to be beneficial to the investigation, but she couldn't think of anything else to do, and if she hadn't come here then the night would just have been spent tossing and turning in bed, getting more and more aggravated that she could not sleep.

So now she found herself standing in front of the cottage again. It was a place she had called home, yet now she was a trespasser. Since it was so late she did not have to worry about the prying eyes of the neighbors, for once. The cottage loomed before her. If it had a soul, would it recognize her as a friend, or would it see her as an intruder? When she had agreed to put the cottage up for sale she had hoped that a family would have a chance to make new memories here, but not memories like this. She had wanted the place to be filled with happiness and love and laughter, things that had been absent here even when she had inhabited the place. Instead there was just a ghostly feeling, a lingering sense of doom, and guilt began to settle in her heart.

Was this all her fault?

She could not escape the thought that this would never have happened had she not agreed to sell the cottage.

She did not get a chance to linger on that matter though, because as soon as she opened the unlocked door and walked a few steps into the house, Jasper growled. His ears pricked up and he moved straight toward the stairs.

Someone else was in the cottage.

Whoever it was might have been there for the same reason as Pippa, but equally it could have been the murderer. Had they come back perhaps to cover up some evidence? Pippa steeled herself and followed Jasper up the stairs. She went carefully, tiptoeing across the plastic sheets. The stairs and the area upstairs had not been changed yet, and she was so familiar that she knew which places would creak under her weight and which ones were safe.

Jasper stood outside the second bedroom, a room that Pippa remembered had been deemed important by Marcus. Was it because Steven had come to stay here? Was this where the murder had taken place?

Pippa opened the door slowly, gently, and peered inside. Her mouth dropped open. It wasn't Steven at all, but instead was the mysterious, waiflike woman she had seen before. Now she was sitting on the bed, hunched up with a timid look on her face, gnawing her lower lip. Pippa blinked and composed herself before she entered the room.

As soon as she made herself known, Pippa startled the woman. She wore a panicked look on her face and rushed to the window, flinging the wide thing open and looking as though she might well toss herself out. Pippa's eyes widened in fear and she reached out, just as she had done with Clive, so afraid that history was going to repeat itself.

"Wait! I'm not here to hurt you! I'm not here to do anything. I'm with the police," Pippa blurted out. The woman was pressed against the wall and she was gripped by fear. It probably didn't help that Jasper was barking. Pippa had to command him to be quiet as he was only scaring the woman.

"My name is Pippa, Pippa Finn, I'm just here trying to find out who killed Marcus Philby. I used to own this cottage. I'm not going to hurt you. If you know something then I suggest that you tell me because I can help you. I can call the constable right now if you like," Pippa reached in her jacket pocket for her phone, but the intense panic on the woman's face grew wider.

"Don't call anyone!" she said in a high pitched, trembling tone. They were the first words she had spoken, and Pippa took that as a breakthrough. Pippa held out her palms and made it clear that she was not going to get her phone.

"Okay, look, it's just you and me. There's nobody else here, and this is Jasper. What's your name?"

The woman looked at her uncertainly and there were a few agonizing moments where Pippa had to wait for a reply, but eventually she learned that the girl's name was Libby. It wasn't the only thing she learned though, because Libby also told Pippa that she was Marcus' daughter.

"I think you had better sit down so that we can talk about this," Pippa said, gesturing to the bed. Libby peeled herself away from the wall and perched on the edge of the bed, looking for all the world as though she was just going to rise again. Tension ran throughout her body and her leg jittered. She bit her nails and kept running her fingers through her hair. "You say that you're his daughter?"

Libby nodded. "But we only found out about each other recently. My mom became sick and that is when she told me... she told me the truth. I found him and I spoke to him. I wasn't sure what I expected really, but he was so kind. He wasn't ashamed of me at all, and he didn't want to turn me away. He wanted to be my family. I had nothing left after Mom died, but he wanted to be a father to me all these years," she became overwhelmed by emotion and almost broke into tears. Pippa tentatively made her way to the bed and sat down behind Libby. It hadn't escaped her notice that Kim and Steven had neglected to mention Libby. Had they known about her too?

"Libby, I'm going to ask you some questions that might be difficult to answer, is that okay?" Pippa asked. Libby nodded. "Did Marcus' family know about this?"

Libby sniffed and shuddered. "Yes they did. That first time we met I told him what had happened and how I had only just learned of him. He made it clear that I wasn't alone and that he wasn't going to abandon me. Mom had never told him about me, and I think he was a little angry that she had kept this from him, but he wasn't angry at me. He just told me that he would take care of me, that he would take care of everything."

"And so he told his family…"

"They didn't like the news. I only heard it from him. He said that they were angry and his marriage was destroyed because his wife didn't want him to be a father to me. He moved out here to get away from the drama and the scandal. I think maybe his wife was afraid that I was just after money, but in truth things would have been easier for him if he had just paid me off. That's not what I wanted though. It's not what either of us wanted."

Pippa took note of the sorrow in Libby's voice. She also noticed that this room was well furnished, especially compared to the rest of the house. She remembered that Harry had told her that Marcus had wanted this room finished first of all. Pippa had wrongly assumed that it had been for Steven. It was actually for Libby.

"So he brought you down here too?"

"He wanted a place for us both to live, a place where we could get to know each other properly."

Pippa knew that this wouldn't have gone down well with Kim, but now that she knew that Libby had been here it shed suspicion on her. Had there been resentment festering throughout her life toward her father? Had there been something rash said and done? It was hard to believe while Libby was sitting there, teetering on the precipice of sorrow, but Pippa knew from experience that murderers came in all shapes and sizes.

"So you've been staying here all this time?" Pippa asked.

"Not the whole time. I didn't like to be here when the construction workers were around. I leave during the day and just explore the area. I come back after they've gone. I don't like to trouble them, and I didn't want them to think badly of Dad... of Marcus," she caught herself. It must have been hard for her to think about what to call him. For most of Libby's life he had been a stranger, and then a father, but had he been a friend as well?

"Libby, you do understand what this means, right? If what you say is true and that you were here then it means you were alone with Marcus. Did you ever feel angry with him? Did he say anything that ever made you feel uncomfortable?"

"Oh no," Libby shook her head vehemently. "He was better than I ever could have imagined. After we met I felt stupid for taking this long to get in touch with him. I wish I had done it sooner. He was so kind to me, just the way I imagined a father always would be, and I wish... I wish I had been able to tell him all of that before it was too late. It wasn't his fault that he had never gotten to know me, and he tried to make up for the lost years as much as he could. I thought we would have more time though. I really thought that this was the beginning of something else but then he died and I..." she began to sob. Her shoulders trembled and Pippa could sense the emotion running through the poor girl. Tears streamed down her cheeks. Pippa saw something in Libby's eyes that was a reflection of her own soul. She knew trauma when she saw it.

"Libby, did you see what happened to your father?" Pippa asked calmly. A sob choked out as Libby nodded. Pippa was about to ask what exactly had happened when her phone rang. She glared at it, but softened when it was Arthur. She held it to her ear and spoke quietly while

Libby gathered herself. At least she was going to have some good news to share with the constable. As it happened, Arthur had some good news as well.

"You need to get down here as soon as possible Pippa. We've just had a confession," he said.

Pippa gently put her hand on Libby's shoulder. "It looks like the truth is going to come out now Libby. Come with me and we'll put this matter to rest. I promise that nothing bad is going to happen to you. Just stay with me and I'll protect you, and on the way you can tell me what happened."

Libby's movements were slow and ponderous, but she moved and was coaxed away by Pippa.

9

P ippa arrived at the station with Libby. Arthur was there to greet her and he had a look of intrigue on his face when he saw Libby.

Pippa made a swift introduction, and left a lot of implied meaning in her words. She took Libby over to a quiet part of the station and got her a cup of tea. She told Libby to stay there for a while until they could take her statement, and then she returned to Arthur.

"She's pretty shaken up. She came here to have a new beginning with her father, and now this happened. She saw it all," Pippa said after she had explained to Arthur the details of what Libby had revealed to her. Arthur wore a dark look and nodded as well.

"It's a grisly affair alright, but at least we have our man."

"Is that just a turn of phrase?" Pippa asked with a half-smile.

"It's the fact Pippa. Steven confessed to everything. He came down here not only to talk to his father about the new living situation, but also about some financial matter. It seems as though they have their affairs tangled in with each other and it's hard to extricate them. There was an argument and things turned violent. According to Steven he was attacked. Kim is trying to get the charges reduced to manslaughter, as Steven only acted in self-defense. It certainly lines up with what we've been told, and I think it's just about as good as we're going to get."

"But it's not the truth Arthur. He's lying to you."

"Why would he lie about killing his father? Even if he gets the sentence reduced to manslaughter instead of murder it's still better than if he just kept quiet. He has no reason to confess otherwise."

"He does Arthur. I know exactly why he's lying. Libby was there. She saw the whole thing."

"Then I think I need to talk with her myself."

Pippa and Arthur were waiting in the interview room. Jasper was by Pippa's side. Libby was elsewhere in the station, hidden from view. Kim and Steven returned. Kim look aggrieved.

"I don't know why you keep bringing us back here when we've told you what you need to know. You have the information you need, so let us be in peace while we're waiting for the wheels of justice to turn. This really is showing how amateur this place is," Kim rolled her eyes and spoke in a bullying, harsh tone. Pippa glared at her with icy eyes. She leaned forward and clasped her hands together so tightly that her knuckles went white.

"New information has come to light that sheds a whole new dimension on this case," she said.

Kim glared at her. There was a slight twitch of her lips and a ripple of unease that passed through her eyes, but she had honed her poker face and so any sign of discomfort was subtle, and only lasted a few seconds. "Well you shouldn't even be here. You may be approved to consult with the police, but I do not believe you have the authority to ask questions here. This is a completely unnecessary meeting. I don't see how there can be any new evidence anyway. My client and his father were the only people there. Since my client is the only person who can tell you what happened there isn't really anything else to add."

"Pippa has the full authority of the police, because I'm the constable of this department and I've granted her that authority. You can see the paperwork for yourself if you like, but in the meantime let's talk about some of the facts of the case because I believe there's something that you've missed." Arthur said, his words clearly rankling Kim, who could do nothing but respect the authority he had earned during his years of service as a police officer.

"We have an eye witness, and this eye witness suggests that it was not Steven here who killed the victim, but you," Pippa let the word linger for a moment. Kim leaned back, flinching as though she had been struck by a whip. Steven's eyes went wide. Pippa tried to leap onto this and spoke to Steven in a terse, hurried tone. "You don't have to take the fall for her Steven. The truth is the only thing that matters. Don't let her get away with this."

"This is ridiculous," Kim slapped the table with her palm, creating a loud sound that ricocheted across the room. She rose to a standing position and gave Pippa and Arthur a withering stare. "I have had quite enough of these dramatics and these utterly unfounded accusations. You're trying to get a rise out of me and I do not appreciate it. This is an incredibly difficult time for me and my son, and we would rather deal with it in private. Steven, let's go. We don't have to put up with this."

"You're going to want to wait to at least see the eye witness," Arthur said, stopping Kim in her tracks. He remained seated while Pippa rose and moved toward the door. She opened it and beckoned Libby in. Libby was still timid, and resembled a mouse as she came forward.

"Why is *she* here?" Kim hissed, jabbing a finger in the air as though it was a sword. It looked as though she wanted to stab Libby directly in the heart. Libby was a few years younger than Steven, an embodiment of Marcus' infidelity, of Kim's failed marriage and her shortcomings as a wife.

"Libby was at the house when the murder happened. She saw everything," Pippa said, placing an arm around Libby's shoulder. She felt Libby's posture straighten as she did so.

Kim's eyes narrowed to the point where her pupils became simple black dots. Her entire body was rigid with tension, like a coiled spring, and the air seemed to crackle and simmer around her, such was the intensity of her anger.

"Her word can't be trusted. She's illegitimate. She's basically an orphan," Kim spoke the words as though they were a curse. She was so angry that she was visibly shaking, and all of the hatred that she had felt for her husband was now passed down to his female progeny. Pippa looked past her though, toward Steven, who cut a solitary figure sitting in his chair. He, too, looked shocked by his mother's outburst.

Arthur held his hands together and spoke slowly. "I think that you might want to calm down Kim. Getting angry is not going to help you in this situation. Your son might have confessed, but what reason does Libby here have to spare him? Her version of events and Steven's do not match up, so the truth must lie somewhere in between. And I think there's something else that doesn't add up.

You see, there's something that has been gnawing at me since you arrived here, like an itch that I simply could not reach. I kept thinking and thinking about it because this case has been elusive for me and it has felt as though there has been a thread that I just haven't been able to tug at. And then it occurred to me. When Steven asked for his lawyer and made the phone call it took you barely any time at all to arrive. I can only imagine that you were so eager to protect him, or yourself, that you lost all thought to detail. While we were waiting here I took the liberty to check on the drive. It was only possible for you to make that time under ideal conditions, and you would have had to have kept a constant pace. I found this quite hard to believe, so I called your practice and they told me that you had indeed been away. According to them you were working from home, but I don't think that's quite accurate. I think you had some business to attend to here, the business of murder."

"That's... that's outrageous," Kim said, although by now she was clearly getting flustered. Her face had paled and beads of sweat appeared on her temples. Her hands turned into fists and then opened again, as though she was trying to grip something that had drifted away from her control.

"Eye witness accounts are notoriously unreliable and even if Libby was at the scene of the crime and can place me there it doesn't mean that I committed the crime. There is no physical evidence, and without that you do not have any case at all. If all you have to rely on is the word of this… girl," she scrunched her face up with derision, "then you have nothing. And that's not even to mention the biggest hole in the story, which is how I would have been able to get his body down to the cave. The truth is that you have nothing, and any lawyer worth her salt is going to tear this testimony to shreds in court. You have your confession and I suggest that you become satisfied with it, because you're not going to get anything else."

The words came thick and fast as Kim switched into her courtroom mode, seeking to bully and push her way through any arguments that would have cast doubt on her innocence. Something still didn't make sense to Pippa though; why would Steven have confessed this if he hadn't committed the crime?

"I think I can help with that?" Steven piped up. All eyes turned to him. He pulled out his phone, scrolling and tapping the screen.

"Steven what are you doing?" Kim asked through gritted teeth. "I don't think this is really necessary. They have all they need."

However, Steven did not pay any attention to her at all. He then held out his phone to Arthur, who noted verbally that it was a bank statement showing a payment made to a boat rental company. At first it didn't seem why this was so important, but then Arthur read out the time. The payment had been made in the afternoon, well before the evening when the murder took place. This pointed to the fact that the crime had been premeditated.

"So this wasn't manslaughter at all," Arthur said, looking toward Steven.

Kim then turned as white as a ghost. Her eyes were two pitted coals, but they burned with fire. "Don't you do this Steven. Don't throw your life away like this. Remember that I've always done everything I could to protect you. How many times have I acted as your counsel? How many times have I kept you from harm? We're together in this life Steven. It's always been you and me."

Steven folded his arms and his chin rested against the top of his chest. He looked sullen, and Pippa wondered if he was going to speak at all.

Then he did. "Except it hasn't, has it? Dad was there too."

"Your father left us the moment he cheated on me. It just took plenty of years for him to own up to the crime."

"But it wasn't just his fault Mom. You were always working late, and when you were at home you weren't really there. You were still on the phone. I was proud of you for being so successful, but the problem is you blamed everything that went wrong in your life on other people. If you had just forgiven him maybe we could have stayed together."

"Forgiven him?" Kim's words were a shriek, so high pitched that even Jasper whimpered. "And do you think we could have ever been happy with her invading our family? I thought we spoke about this Steven. He raised you. You were the one who deserved what was in his will, not her."

Pippa felt her stomach clench. Yet again there was a dispute about a will.

Steven turned away from Kim and looked directly at Arthur. "I can't do this anymore. I would like to recant my statement as I was given faulty advice by my attorney. I have something else to say," he said, all the while Kim was gnashing her teeth and looking more feral by the moment. In the end Arthur had to get her taken out of the room so that Steven could speak without being interrupted, and without Kim trying to keep him silent.

Kim's presence had brought a ringing to Pippa's ears, but that was subsiding after Kim was removed from the room. Libby remained though, and Steven was still at the table. His voice was low and slow as he recounted the events of what happened.

"Mom was right, I didn't want to share, but I don't blame Libby for that. It's not her fault. It was a shock at the time. I knew things weren't perfect between Mom and Dad, but when this happened it was clear there was no coming back from it. I tried though. All I wanted was for them to stay together. I thought if I could just talk some sense into them then maybe there would be a chance. But then Dad had to go and buy a cottage out here. The more time he spent out here the more real it seemed, and I knew that if I was going to convince him to come back then it had to be soon. The only mistake I made was in telling Mom that I was coming down here. She made everything worse. I didn't think anything of it at the time, but she told me to rent a boat that day so we could go sailing off the coast. I didn't even think she had murder in mind, not until it happened..." he trailed off then and went quiet. "I hoped that since they were in the same room with each other they might be able to talk things out, but Mom had no intention of doing it. I watched them as they just argued and argued with each other, and it was clear that nothing was going to bring them back together. We left and I thought that was the end of it.

Then later on I got a call from Mom. I could tell that something was wrong from the start. She told me that Dad had died and she needed help moving the body. It was always matter of fact with her. I was in shock. I didn't know what to do, but Mom always did. It's what she was good at. So I did what I always did, I followed her orders. She convinced me that it would be best for both of us if we got rid of the body. She was insulted and angry because of Libby."

Pippa glanced to Libby, who nodded a little. This matched up with what she said, although Libby hadn't mentioned Steven being there. "Libby, did you see Steven as well?"

Libby shook her head. "I left as soon as it happened. I was afraid she would find me as well. I didn't know who to turn to or anything, and I thought even if I called the police Kim would just find a way to twist things in her favor. Marcus said that was always what she was good at. I was so scared. I wanted to run, but I had nowhere else to go. I just had to hide during the day and stay at the cottage in the nighttime hours."

"Why did you confess to the crime if you knew it wasn't the truth?" Arthur asked Steven.

Steven leaned back and shrugged. "Mom has always known what to do. It probably doesn't come as a shock to you to know that I'm no angel, but Mom has always managed to get me off the hook. She said that I owed her one, and if I didn't then she could cut all the strings she had attached to the different parts of my life. She also told me that it was in both our best interests for me to take the fall. She said if the truth came out then she would be disbarred and she'd never be able to work again, and I would be in trouble for helping her anyway. She told me that there was no point for us both to get in trouble, and she could use her skills as a lawyer to get the sentence reduced and reduced until I barely had to serve any time at all. She also said that she would make sure it didn't affect me in a professional sense, and that as long as she kept working as a lawyer she would be able to support the same lifestyle we were used to. She's always had a way of speaking that makes her way seem the right way, and I suppose that I was in so much shock that I just went along with it.

I got the boat ready on the shore and then helped her with the body. We had to use a wheelbarrow to carry Dad to the car, and then took that down to the beach. We covered him in tarpaulin. I worried that someone was going to see us, but Mom said that this place wasn't like London. There weren't always people watching. We saw the caves and put him there, intending to get rid of the body properly later. We didn't want to just put him at sea in case he washed up on the shore. Mom wedged the tip of the screwdriver into a rock and let it sink in the water. Then she said that we should stay in the area for a couple of days until we could get the body. I went to the only place that was open and got a drink. I just... I needed to do something to get the thoughts out of my mind. It didn't really sink in that this had just happened. And then you guys came and found me and Mom kept telling me that everything was alright, that they could never find out the truth, but I suppose she never saw you coming," he turned and spoke to Libby when he said this. His eyes were watery, but his attention was drawn back to Arthur.

"Steven, you do understand that although your testimony is going to help us, you will not be acquitted for abetting a murderer. But whatever punishment you receive, it's not going to be as bad as it would have been had you stuck to your previous confession."

Steven nodded mutely and his face looked drawn. "I know that this is what has to be done. I just wish it hadn't happened in the first place. It's like this whirlwind has just taken over my life and it's ruined everything."

But it wasn't a whirlwind, Pippa thought, it was just a woman who could not cope with the idea that her husband had another child. And something else that Steven had said made her think as well. On the beach he noted how Kim had said that nobody was watching out here, but that wasn't true at all. God was always watching.

10

A couple of weeks had passed since the truth had emerged. A surly Kim had been arrested, while Steven was taken in for questioning and punished for abetting the crime. Libby had remained in Burlybottom on Sea, and she found it more comfortable to be around the work crew. Pippa had visited her during walks with Jasper. This time, to get away from the noise of hammering and drilling, Libby had joined them on a walk past the cottage, heading toward the church.

"How are you today?" Pippa asked.

"I'm okay. I have good days and bad days. I'm just glad it's all over really, but I don't think I'll ever forget that moment of seeing him being stabbed. It all happened so suddenly and I wish I could have done something to stop it, but it was like I was frozen."

"I know exactly what you mean," Pippa said, wishing that she didn't, but she thought that even if it was sobering that these things should happen, it was good that there were people who had been through the same things and could empathize with each other. "Have you decided whether you're going to stay yet?"

"I don't know... when I came here I thought it was the most beautiful place, but I think that was because I was finally going to get a chance to get to know my dad. He had such great plans for him and I. It wasn't easy for him, you know, losing his family. He wanted it to work out, but it just wasn't going to happen. Not with Kim being the way she is. I never wanted to make them feel bad either. She treated me like I was a sin. Maybe I am."

"No you're not. What your father might have done was a sin, but you're not a sin just because you were the outcome of it. Life can never be a sin. It's just a shame life has to be so complicated."

"Yes, it is. Speaking of complicated; I've been writing to Steven."

"Oh?"

Libby nodded. "I still feel like there's so much I don't know about my father. Steven was fortunate enough to have a whole life with him, so if I'm ever going to know about Dad there's only one person who I can learn that from. Besides, he is my brother as well. I feel like I ought to stick with family seeing as how he's the only family I have now."

"That might be true in one sense, but one thing I've learned about being in Burlybottom on Sea is that there are a lot of people willing to become a part of your family. And there's that place as well, a place where you're never going to feel alone," Pippa lifted her hand and pointed to the sight of the steeple that emerged from between the trees. It filled her heart with a sense of relief and comfort, and by the look on Libby's face, she felt the same thing.

"I'll stay around for a little while at least because I don't have anywhere else to go, but I don't know if I can stay in the cottage. I just don't know if I deserve a place that nice."

Pippa smiled. "That is a building that has seen its share of sorrow over the years, but it's also seen plenty of happy memories too. It deserves a chance to have some more made there, and I think you deserve a chance to make some too. I think you should stay there. I'm sure it's what your father would have wanted."

"Yeah, maybe he did," Libby said. The two women walked on in tandem, reflecting on the people they had lost and what was left in front of them. Pippa realized in that moment that she wasn't sorry she no longer had the cottage, because she was quite happy in her new home near Jack. And she was glad to know that the cottage would be inhabited by someone sweet, someone who wanted to make a new home for themselves. Burlybottom on Sea seemed like a place for lost souls who all gravitated together and found each other in this humble coastal town.

And Pippa felt as though she had found herself again as well. Investigating this murder had reminded her that she was capable of making a difference in people's lives. It had filled her with a vigor she had been missing, and had improved her mood greatly. She knew that there was nothing she could do to change the past or prevent bad things from happening, but she could help the victims find justice at least, and she could remember those who had passed before her. But the best tribute she could make to them, to Clive and to Granddad and to all the other people she had lost, was to live well and enjoy every moment she was given as much as she possibly could.

She entered the church and smiled at the Reverend as she made her way to the front. She fell to her knees and clasped her hands in prayer. She reflected on her relationship with her grandfather. She prayed for peace for those souls who had been thrust into heaven before their time, and then she prayed for strength and courage for what she was about to do. There was something she needed to do that she had been putting off for too long, allowing other things to get in the way, but she could not be ruled by fear.

It was time to tell Jack that she loved him.

THANK YOU FOR CHOOSING A PUREREAD BOOK!

We hope you enjoyed the story, and as a way to thank you for choosing PureRead we'd like to send you this free Special Edition Cozy, and other fun reader rewards…

Click Here to download your free Cozy Mystery
PureRead.com/cozy

Thanks again for reading.

See you soon!

OTHER BOOKS IN THIS SERIES

Read them all...

If you loved this story why not continue straight away with other books in the series?

Inheriting A Mystery

The Secrets of the Sea

Mystery on the Doorstep

Hammer Home A Mystery

Three Salty Secrets

Death on Aisle Five

Dead & Breakfast

Family Secrets & Canine Conundrums

OUR GIFT TO YOU

AS A WAY TO SAY THANK YOU WE WOULD
LOVE TO SEND YOU THIS SPECIAL EDITION
COZY MYSTERY FREE OF CHARGE.

Our Reader List is 100% FREE

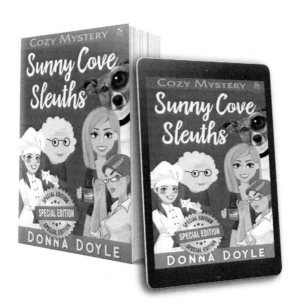

Click Here to download your free Cozy Mystery
PureRead.com/cozy

At PureRead we publish books you can trust. Great tales without smut or swearing, but with all of the mystery and romance you expect from a great story.

Be the first to know when we release new books, take part in our fun competitions, and get surprise free books in your inbox by signing up to our Reader list.

As a thank you you'll receive this exclusive Special Edition Cozy available only to our subscribers...

Click Here to download your free Cozy Mystery
PureRead.com/cozy

Thanks again for reading.
See you soon!

Made in United States
North Haven, CT
04 February 2025

65389127R00059